IS 61 LIBRARY

The Elevator Family

The Elevator Family

Douglas Evans

A Yearling Book

35 Years of Exceptional Reading

Yearling Books
Established 1966

Published by
Dell Yearling
an imprint of
Random House Children's Books
a division of Random House, Inc.
1540 Broadway
New York, New York 10036

Visit us on the Web! www.randomhouse.com/kids
Educators and librarians, for a variety of teaching
tools, visit us at www.randomhouse.com/teachers

ISBN: 0-440-41650-7

Reprinted by arrangement with Delacorte Press

Printed in the United States of America

July 2001

10

OPM

To my mother and father

The doors slid open. The four Wilsons stepped into the little room. They dropped their suitcases and backpacks on the floor.

"Splendid! A gem of a place," said Walter Wilson. "The kind woman at the front desk said the hotel is full, but here's this first-rate room. And it appears to be vacant." He pulled out his suspenders with his thumbs and snapped them on his broad chest. "Only the best for this family. Nothing less will do."

Winona Wilson, Walter's wife, turned a complete circle. "A full-length mirror, a telephone, wall-to-wall carpeting. And listen." Soft marimba music floated down from the ceiling. "How lovely!"

"And look at all those buttons!" said Winslow Wilson, age ten. He pressed one button marked Close, and the doors slid shut. "Fantabulous!"

The little room vibrated slightly. A high-pitched hum came from overhead. "We're moving," said Winslow's twin sister, Whitney. "We're gliding upward. I wonder where we're going."

Walter crossed his fingers over his sizable belly. "A mobile room with all these extras," he said. "I say we take this fine room for our vacation. I say we move right in."

"Hear! Hear!" said the others.

The doors slid open. In the hallway stood

an elderly couple holding suitcases. They remained still and mute while the four Wilsons waved to them.

"Greetings, fellow travelers," Walter called out.

"I'm so sorry," said Winona. "We just decided to take this room."

"But I think the room next door is vacant," said Winslow.

"It was on the first floor, but it might have moved by now," said Whitney.

The doors shut and the room started to drop. It opened again in the hotel's vast marble lobby. In the doorway stood a teenage boy wearing a wrinkled red jacket and a white shirt buttoned too tightly around his neck. Behind him stood two trunks.

"Splendid, young man," said Walter. "I wondered where you went. Wheel those trunks right in here. We'll take this room for three nights if it's available."

The teenager pushed the trunks forward.

His black bow tie bobbed up and down on his Adam's apple as he spoke. "Sir? You want *this* room, sir? I don't understand, sir."

"The room needs a few items—bed linen and towels and whatnot," said Winona. "But it's small and cozy, just the way we like it. We're a close-knit family."

"This room's about the size of the van we drove to Alaska last summer," said Winslow. "Two thousand miles . . . one month together."

Whitney leaned against a trunk. "And last Christmas we stayed in a small fishing hut on the ice in Minnesota," she said. "I just hope Winslow keeps his socks clean this time."

The teenager raked his fingers through his hair. "Well, I'm only a bellhop. I don't make the rules around here."

"But tell us your name, young man," Walter said.

"Gavin, sir."

"Well, Gavin," said Walter, "you've given

us excellent service. Stop in anytime. Guests are always welcome in our home."

Gavin shrugged. "Whatever," he said. "I've seen stranger things in this hotel, that's for sure."

"One more thing," Winona called as the bellhop started to leave. "Could you tell us the number of our mobile room?"

The teenager shrugged again. "I'm not sure, ma'am."

Winslow pointed to the button panel next to the doors. "Look at that tag," he said.

"Our room doesn't have a number," said Whitney "It has a name."

"'Otis!'" the four Wilsons read together.

The doors slid shut, and the little room started moving again.

T he little room traveled upward. It went down, and it shot up again.

"First things first," said Winona. "We must put Otis in order."

Walter rolled up his shirtsleeves and rubbed his palms together. "Come on, everyone," he said. "Help me with the trunks."

Together the Wilsons tipped the trunks on

their sides and pushed them against the walls. The leather lids would serve as comfortable beds.

The doors opened on the tenth floor. The family looked down a hallway with red roses adorning the wallpaper.

"How lovely," said Winona. "At every stop our room gives us a different view."

By the doorway Winslow spotted a small round table. Ignoring the stare of the tall man in a tuxedo standing there, he grabbed the piece of furniture. He pulled it into the room before the doors closed again.

Otis rose to the fourteenth floor. There Whitney found two folding chairs. "Just what we need," she said, and claimed them as well.

On the twenty-first floor Winona discovered a cart stacked with towels and sheets. "I don't think the maid would mind if we made up our own beds today," she said. She grabbed some sheets, towels, and little bars of soap and raced back into the room before the doors slid shut.

As a final touch, Walter unzipped a suitcase and pulled out a framed sampler. Stitched by Whitney and Winslow before they could spell very well, the sampler displayed the words Home Sweat Home. With a thumbtack, Walter proudly hung it on the wall.

"A family tradition," he announced. "'Home Sweat Home' hangs wherever the Wilsons stay. Only the best for our family. Nothing less will do."

By the time the doors opened on the top floor of the hotel, Otis looked homey and complete. Walter was leaning back in a chair, doing a crossword puzzle in the newspaper. Winona sat in the other chair, sketching the twins in her sketchbook, while Whitney and Winslow were sprawled on the trunk-beds, reading paperback books.

After the little room took several more

trips up and down, Walter snapped his newspaper and said, "Lunchtime. Let's call room service to deliver our meal."

Winona studied the button panel. "The bottom button is marked *L*," she said. "Perhaps that stands for *lunch*." She pressed the button with her thumb and the little room dropped.

The doors opened in the hotel lobby. Gavin stood in the doorway with a food trolley by his side.

"Excellent service, young man," said Walter. "Lunch is waiting for us, right on the button. Wheel that cart on in here. We will be eating lunch in our room today."

"But, sir, I was taking this food up to the seventh floor," said the bellhop.

"It doesn't matter what floor we eat on, Gavin," said Winona. "In our mobile room we can eat on any floor we want."

With a shrug, the teenager pushed the trolley into the room. With another shrug, he turned on his heel and stepped back into the lobby.

The doors closed behind him.

As the room rose, Winona laid dishes and silverware out on the table. She lifted the lid off a serving dish and announced, "Spaghetti!"

Walter tucked a napkin into his collar. After inspecting the label on a bottle of red wine, he pulled the cork. "Only the best," he said. He poured a glass for Winona and one for himself. The twins had grape juice.

Ping! Ping! Ping! went Walter's fork against his glass.

"I propose a toast," he said. "Here's to our new home."

The family raised their glasses. "Hear! Hear!" they said in unison. "To Otis!"

No sooner had the four Wilsons started slurping spaghetti than the doors opened on the twenty-fourth floor. Into the little room stepped a brown-haired man. He carried a brown briefcase. He wore a brown business suit, brown shoes, and a brown tie. After pressing the *L* button, he stood stiffly with his back toward the Wilsons and his briefcase against his stomach. A dab of shaving cream, apparently missed while he shaved that morning, jiggled behind his ear.

Walter tapped a napkin against his lips. "Kind of you to drop in, sir," he called out. "Guests are always welcome in our home."

"People don't need to walk up and down stairs to visit us," said Winona. "Our room rises and lowers to visit them."

The man remained silent and rigid. As the doors closed, they banged against his briefcase and bounced open again.

"Fantabulous," said Winslow.

The man took a short step backward and let the doors slide past him. He turned his head and squinted at the beds. He smiled toward Home Sweat Home on the wall, the table, and the family dining around it. "You folks living in here?" he asked.

Walter spun his fork in his spaghetti. "Just moved in," he said. "We're lucky to have grabbed Otis early. Every time we stop, people are standing outside the doors, waiting to take it."

The man wiped his brow with a sleeve. "No kidding?" he said. "So what's it like?"

"It has its ups . . . ," said Whitney.

"And downs," said Winslow.

"We noticed that you pressed the lunch button as we did," said Winona. "Please have a seat and join us. There's plenty of spaghetti for everyone."

"Winslow, scoot over," said Walter. "Give our guest some room."

The man nodded and sat down with his briefcase on his lap. "The name's Bob Brown," he said. "I appreciate the invitation. Gets a bit lonely on the road. Most often I sit alone, eat alone, and walk the streets alone. I guess that's the way the world works."

Walter poured the man some wine. Winona dished out a plate of spaghetti for him.

"Funny thing," the man went on. "On my job I talk to dozens of people each day. I pass thousands more on the sidewalk. Yet I still spend much of my time alone. No kidding. It seems the more people there are around, the harder they are to meet."

Winslow wiped his mouth with the back of his hand. "So what do you do, Mr. Brown?" he asked.

"I'm a fad salesman, son. I deal in fads. I travel around the country putting the latest fad in stores."

"You mean like virtual pets and Pet Rocks?" asked Winslow.

"Beanie dolls and Mexican jumping beans?" said Whitney.

"I've loaded all those fads on shelves, kids," said the salesman. "Also super balls, super bubbles, super putty, and super squirt guns—fads come and go. Trouble is, once I get the stores filled with one item, I gotta start traveling again to fill them with another. One month smelly stickers will be a hot item; the next, children will only buy smelly pens."

Walter gulped some pasta. "That means you're often away from your family," he said.

"No kidding," said Mr. Brown. "I miss my wife and daughter an awful lot. Someday I hope to think up a fad idea myself that will be such a hit I'll never need to leave home again. But for now I must stay on the road. That's the way the world works."

A half hour later the doors slid open in the hotel lobby. Mr. Brown stepped out, pushing the food trolley stacked with empty plates. "I'm off to sell the latest fad to the toy stores in this city," he said. "Pencil suckers. Kids can suck on one end while writing stories with the other. Thanks for the lunch. It was great."

The four Wilsons waved.

"Only the best for this family," said Walter.

"Stop in anytime," Winona added. "Guests are always welcome in Otis."

4

The little room remained in the hotel lobby. Walter Wilson returned to his crossword puzzle; Winona resumed sketching; Whitney read her paperback, while Winslow sat in the doorway, letting the doors close and bounce open against his sneaker, close and bounce, close and bounce.

This peaceful scene was suddenly disturbed when screams exploded from the front door of the hotel. Shortly afterward, two men with long hair and a woman with short hair burst into the little room. All three wore black leather shirts, pants, and boots. All three were so busy huffing and puffing, they failed to notice the four Wilsons sitting there. Frantically the woman smacked a button on the panel with her palm. Winslow stood to let the doors slide past him, and the noise in the lobby became muffled.

The taller of the men wiped his neck with a red bandanna. "Whoa! Wow! Whee!" he said. "They're getting closer all the time. Someday they're going to catch us. What then?"

"Those fans nearly tore me shirt right off me back," said the shorter man. "One grabbed me hair. Another ripped me jacket."

The woman slumped to the floor. "Twelve more cities!" she exclaimed. "A dozen more times we must go through this rigamarole. Then we can go home."

As the little room started upward, Walter lowered his newspaper. "Splendid. More company," he said.

Winona set down her sketchpad. She placed her hand on the woman's forehead. "You look frazzled, dear," she said. "I hope you don't have a fever."

The three newcomers stared at the Wilsons.

"Whoa! Wow! Whee!" went the tall man. "More people! We can't escape them."

"Please, no more autographs?" said the short man. "Me hand is killing me from writing me name so many times."

"Sit down and sit tight," said Walter. "We're the Wilsons, and who may you be?"

The tall man sat on the edge of a trunk. "*What?*" he answered.

"What is your name?" asked Winona.

"That's right," said the short man, sitting down on the other trunk.

Whitney looked up from her paperback. "You're *What*?"

"Fantabulous," said Winslow. "You're the rock band called What?"

Walter looked at his newspaper. "Why, here's your picture in the entertainment section," he said. "It says What is playing a concert in the city tonight."

"That's right," the woman sighed.

Winona pointed to the speaker overhead. Soft harp music filled the room. "We have our own piped-in music," she said.

The tall man nodded. "And that music's rather nice," he said. "This is the most peaceful place we've been in all day."

"Certainly," said the short man. "After riding all week in big limousines, playing in big concert halls, and staying in big hotel rooms, this place is a relaxing change."

The woman closed her eyes. "All the loud

music," she said. "All the noisy traffic. All the screaming fans. I almost forgot what quiet is like."

The three visitors said no more. Walter returned to his puzzle. Winona started sketching, and the twins read their paperbacks.

As the little room continued on its never-ending journey, the musicians sat still and quiet. For more than an hour they rode up and down, up and down, up and down.

After the rock musicians left, the doors opened in the lobby. The bellhop stood in the doorway.

"Gavin!" the Wilsons called out.

The teenager's head was bent and his bow tie crooked. By his side he held a bouquet of daffodils.

"You look down in the dumps, young man," said Walter. "Come on in. Come on in."

Gavin stepped into the little room. The doors slid closed, and Otis started upward.

Winona, busy thumbtacking her sketches to the walls, paused to place her palm on Gavin's forehead. "What's wrong, dear?" she said. "You don't have a fever."

Gavin held out the daffodils. "These are for you, Mrs. Wilson," he mumbled. "I sure hope you like flowers."

Winona dropped the bouquet into a glass on the small round table. "They're beautiful, Gavin," she said. "But wouldn't you rather give them to a girl you admire?"

Gavin sat down on the trunk. His bow tie bobbed up and down on his Adam's apple. "That's the problem, Mrs. Wilson. Those flowers *came* from a girl I admire."

Whitney set down her paperback. "You mean the girl in the flower stall across the lobby?" she asked.

"She waves to us whenever Otis is parked down there," said Winslow.

Gavin's face turned the same red as his jacket. "Sure. Cathy's her name. And I've bought so many flowers from her stall in the past week that my apartment is beginning to look as if I died or something."

"Young man," said Walter, "I believe you have something that's commonly called a crush."

Gavin blushed some more. Then, realizing he was blushing, he turned an even deeper red.

"So you like Cathy, but you are too shy to speak to her," said Winona. "Is that why you keep buying flowers from her?"

Gavin nodded. "A girl like Cathy would never want to go on a date with someone like me, that's for sure. I'm just a bellhop. I don't make much money. I'm saving up to go to college next year, but then I'll be even poorer."

"But you're an excellent bellhop, Gavin," said Winona.

"The best," said Walter. "You're only going up in this world, young man."

At that moment the little room began to drop, and the teenager sighed.

The doors reopened in the hotel lobby. Cathy stood in her stall, snipping roses. She was a pretty girl with a long brown ponytail.

The Wilsons waved to her, and she waved back.

Gavin combed his fingers through his hair. "It's hopeless," he said "I'll never get up enough nerve to talk to her." He stepped out of the little room, shaking his head.

"We'll discuss this more in the morning, young man," said Walter. "Could we have breakfast delivered at seven?"

Gavin shrugged. "Sure," he said. Then he slunk across the lobby without once looking toward the flower stall.

At five o'clock that evening Walter drummed his fingers on his belly. "Let's call out for pizza," he said "We'll eat in Otis tonight."

"Pepperoni!" Winona cried.

"Mushrooms!" declared Whitney.

"Anchovies!" said Winslow.

Walter picked up the white telephone on

the wall. "I'll order an extra large with every-thing on it," he said.

"Hello," said a voice on the phone. It was Mrs. Quinn, the hotel receptionist.

"Evening, madam," said Walter. "We would like to order a pizza."

"Sir, that's not a real telephone you're using," Mrs. Quinn said crossly.

"A phony phone?" said Walter. "How can one tell a phony phone from a telephone?"

There followed mutters and muffled voices, until Gavin's voice came on the line. "Mr. Wilson? Can I help you?"

"Splendid, young man," said Walter. "Connect us with the best pizza place you know."

"Sure, sir," said Gavin.

In a matter of seconds, a man's voice on the phone said, "Hello, Peace Pizza Parlor. Pizza slices at peaceful prices."

"Please deliver your largest pizza with the

works on it," said Walter. "We're staying at the San Francisco Hotel."

"What floor?" asked the pizza man.

"We're in the Otis Room, so it depends on what time you show up," answered Walter. "Floor eleven, perhaps fifteen. We've been on floor twenty a lot lately."

A half hour later the doors of the little room opened in the lobby. A boy wearing a green baseball cap and a T-shirt with a peace sign on the front stood at the reception desk. He held a pizza box on his palm like a waiter. Mrs. Quinn scowled as she pointed to the Wilsons.

The boy jogged over to Otis. He placed the pizza on the little table, looking around. "You know, I've delivered pizzas to picnic grounds, hospital rooms, fire stations, and battleships in the bay," he said. "But this is a first."

Walter handed the boy a twenty-dollar

bill. "Only the best for our family," he said. "Nothing less will do. Keep the change."

Soon the aromas of cheese, olives, anchovies, mushrooms, sausage, and tomatoes filled the little room.

Walter wiggled his fingers and said, "Age before beauty. I'll take the first slice."

"Ladies before gentlemen!" called Winona. "The first piece should be mine."

"Children first!" cried the twins, and they all dove for the pizza at the same time.

While the ceiling played a bouncy Beatles tune, the Wilsons munched their pizza. Soon only one slice remained.

"I've invented a game to see who gets that last piece of Peace Pizza," said Winona.

She pointed to the row of numbers above the sliding doors.

L 1 2 3 4 5 6 7 8 9 10 11
12 14 15 16 17 18 19 20 21 22
23 24 25 26 27 28 29 30 31 32 33 34

As Otis journeyed up and down, a number would light up to show what floor the little room was on.

"Otis is now stopped on the sixteenth floor," Winona went on. "Whoever can guess the next floor it will stop at gets the last slice. I guess floor nineteen."

"What happened to floor thirteen?" asked Winslow.

Walter snapped his suspenders. "Many hotels consider it bad luck to have a thirteenth floor," he explained. "But I feel lucky right now and think we'll start going down. Our next stop will be the twelfth floor."

"Floor twenty-four," guessed Winslow. "That's Mr. Brown's floor, and it's time for him to go out to dinner."

"We'll stop on the top floor," Whitney predicted. "Number thirty-four."

The Wilsons waited in silence. Soon the little room started moving upward.

Walter waved sadly to the pizza slice. "Good-bye, my beauty," he said.

One by one the numbers above the doors blinked on and off.

17 . . . 18 . . . 19 . . . 20 . . .

Winona snapped her fingers. "I lose," she said.

21 . . . 22 . . . 23 . . . 24 . . . 25 . . .

"I'm out," said Winslow.

26 . . . 27 . . . 28 . . . 29 . . . 30 . . .

"Go! Go! Go!" shouted Whitney.

31 . . . 34 . . . and the doors slid open.

Whitney grinned. "Well," she said. "I guess that last piece of Peace Pizza is mine." And triumphantly she leaned forward to grab it.

On the thirty-fourth floor stood a woman with white hair. She wore a white track suit and white running shoes and held a small white poodle. As she stepped into the little room her diamond earrings flashed in the overhead light.

The woman smiled at the Wilsons and pressed the *L* button. "My, my, Oui-Oui," she whispered to her dog. "I heard there's a shortage of hotel rooms in this city, but I had no idea the problem was this bad."

Walter lowered his newspaper. "Greetings, madam," he said. "Welcome to Otis, our humble vacation home."

"My, my," repeated the woman. "You're on vacation? Are you comfortable in here?"

"It has its ups . . . ," said Whitney.

"And downs," said Winslow.

"We are the Wilson family," said Winona.

"I'm Abigail Goldengate," said the woman. She rubbed the dog behind the ears. "And this little fella is Oui-Oui."

"Yap! Yap! Yap!" went the dog.

"Goldengate?" said Winslow. "Didn't they name a bridge in this city after you?"

"They named the bridge after my late husband, Gordon Goldengate," the woman replied. "Since he departed this world, I've been living on the top floor of this hotel."

"Then please join us, Abigail," said

Winona. "We'll call room service for some coffee and cookies."

"I wish I had time. But I must rush off," said the woman. "If I don't fit in time to keep fit at the hotel's fitness center, I have a fit."

The doors opened in the lobby, and the woman hurried away.

For the next hour the Wilsons played Pick-Up Sticks. Winslow won game one and game two. He was about to pinch a blue stick to win game three when the doors opened again on the top floor. Into the room stepped Mrs. Goldengate. Now she wore a white pantsuit and a white scarf. A diamond broach sparkled on her lapel.

"Yap! Yap! Yap!" went Oui-Oui in her arms.

"Welcome back, madam," said Walter. "I thought we left you down below."

"As part of my workout routine, I prefer to jog up the stairs," the woman replied. She rubbed the poodle under his neck. "This little fella also gets some exercise."

"Come join our game of Pick-Up Sticks, Abigail," said Winona. "Winslow is clobbering us all. I think he'll make an excellent brain surgeon someday."

"Or a pickpocket," said Whitney.

"I wish I had time," said Mrs. Goldengate. "But I must rush out again. I'm dining at the hotel restaurant, and I'm late already."

Even before the doors had opened fully, the woman raced out.

Walter shook his head. "Watching her is like watching a video on fast forward," he said.

"I have a feeling we'll see her again soon," said Winona.

Sure enough, after five more games of Pick-Up Sticks, Mrs. Goldengate reentered the little room with a dab of mustard on her cheek. She rode with the Wilsons up to the top floor. She returned shortly wearing a white dress and a diamond necklace.

"Yap! Yap! Yap!" went the poodle in her arms.

"Rush, rush, rush," the woman said. "Now I'm off to a hot nightspot I spotted where one goes to be spotted. But I first need to drop Oui-Oui off at the dog-sitter's."

Walter looked at Winona, Winona at Winslow, Winslow at Whitney, and Whitney at Walter.

"Madam, we can sit your pooch for you," Walter said.

The woman placed her poodle on a trunk and checked her watch. "Oh, that would save me so much time," she said. "Look at the time now. I wish I had time to chat, but there's no time." The doors opened, and she flew across the lobby.

The moment the Wilsons resumed their game of Pick-Up Sticks, Oui-Oui curled up on the trunk and was quiet.

The room went up.

The room went down.

Not until midnight, however, did Mrs. Goldengate return. She sat on the end of a trunk and yawned. Oui-Oui climbed into her lap and fell asleep.

"I can't stay long" said the woman. "I must get up early for a book-club meeting and a garden-club meeting, followed by a golf-club club meeting at the country club. Rush, rush, rush. That's all I seem to do. Rush, rush, rush."

Winona put her palm on the woman's forehead. "Your face is so pale, Abigail," she said.

"We know you've had a busy evening," said Whitney.

Mrs. Goldengate closed her eyes. "But to tell you the truth, I was so busy rushing around I can't remember much of anything. It's all one big blur. My, this is a peaceful place."

When the little room reached the top floor, the woman remained sitting on the trunk. The Wilsons played a last quiet game of Pick-

Up Sticks before the twins helped the woman down the hallway to her room.

"Time for bed. We have a big day tomorrow," Walter announced a short time later.

Soon Winona, Winslow, and Whitney, dressed in their pajamas, were snuggled under quilts on the trunk-beds. Walter, however, stood by the doors, studying the button panel.

"All those buttons," he said. "But not one works the light."

He stood on a chair and spit on his fingers. Reaching up, he turned the lightbulb in the ceiling. "Lights out," he said. And the little room turned inky black.

Bumps, crashes, and faint curses came from the darkness as Walter groped his way to bed.

"Good night, family," he finally called out.

"Sweet dreams," said Winona.

"Sleep tight," the family said together.

8

The next morning the Wilsons awoke to the soft hum of Otis's motor. Even before they rolled out of bed, they received their first visitors. On the twentieth floor, Tom and Tia Twiddle, two tourists from Texas, entered Otis toting trunks.

Walter sat up. He pulled his pajama top over his belly. "Top of the morning, folks," he said.

Whether the Twiddles were shy or felt embarrassed at disturbing the sleeping family, the Wilsons never knew. But the couple remained silent all the way down to the lobby. When the doors opened, they stepped out without a wave or a nod.

"Rise and shine, family," Walter called out. "Let's get up and at 'em."

As he spoke, Otis dropped some more. This time the doors opened in the hotel basement. The Wilsons had a startling view of steaming pipes, hissing water heaters, and silver ducts that spread across the ceiling. Switches and fuse boxes covered the walls.

Leaning against a door frame, his eyes half shut, was the night watchman. A patch on his shirt pocket said his name was Joe. Joe yawned as he stepped into the little room and punched the L button.

"Morning," the four Wilsons said in unison.

"That's good," the man mumbled. The

brim of his hat rose an inch as he leaned against the wall. His head remained down as the little room returned to the lobby and he stepped out.

After the doors closed, the Wilsons changed into running shorts, T-shirts, and sneakers. In single file, they jogged out of the little room. Walter led the way. With his fists against his chest and his thumbs pointing upward, he ran across the lobby. Mrs. Quinn frowned as the family passed the reception desk.

Roland, the doorman, dressed in a blue uniform and a gold-braided hat, held the front door open. "Cab, sir?" he asked Walter.

"No, thank you, Roland," Walter replied. "It's a bracing morning. We're going out for a bit of exercise."

Twenty minutes later Roland reopened the hotel door. The Wilsons, now shiny with sweat, jogged back into the hotel.

Gavin was waiting in the little room. A cart carrying breakfast and the morning newspaper stood by his side. He held out a bouquet of carnations. "Here, Mrs. Wilson," he said glumly.

"Oh, dear," said Winona. "Still have that problem, Gavin?"

"Sure do," the teenager replied. With a shrug, he stepped outside.

All morning long the little room moved up and down. Time after time the doors opened and the Wilsons welcomed visitors.

Shortly after breakfast a Japanese family entered Otis.

"Fascinating. Fascinating," they said. The husband took out a video camera and taped the Wilsons and their mobile room until the doors opened again.

Next the Bayleys from England stopped by. They took a trip upward several floors.

"We call these rooms lifts back home,"

said Mrs. Bayley. "But no one remains in them more than a minute or two."

"You Yanks have the most brilliant ideas," said Mr. Bayley.

When the little room returned to the lobby, Gavin entered. He handed Winona some sunflowers. "Next time I'll talk to her for sure," he said. He made an about-face and left.

But when the doors opened a half hour later, Gavin stood there holding a dozen roses. "Here, Mrs. Wilson," he muttered. "Next time. Next time I'll do it."

An hour later, however, he showed up with daisies, and soon after that he brought in a basket of petunias. By now blooms crowded every corner of Otis. Although the place smelled wonderful, the Wilsons were running out of space to sit. Something had to be done.

That evening Walter called out for a

bucket of chicken. A girl dressed in a chicken outfit delivered it a half hour later. As the Wilsons ate, they discussed Gavin's problem.

"The boy reminds me of me when I first saw your mother," Walter said to the twins. "I was so tongue-tied it took me six months to work up the nerve to talk to her."

"And that was only when we got locked in the school coat closet together by accident," said Winona.

Walter waved a drumstick in the air. "Ah, that small place was wonderful."

"We liked it so much we talked for hours before shouting for help," Winona added.

"What Gavin needs is an opportunity away from work to speak with Cathy," said Winslow.

Whitney tossed a chicken bone into the bucket. "Then why not have a party for them?" she said. "We could have it right here in Otis."

"Yes, a dinner party," said Winona. "We'll

invite Cathy and Gavin and all our friends from the hotel."

Walter wiped his greasy fingers on a napkin. "Splendid idea. How about tomorrow night? In the morning we'll ask Michelle, the hotel chef, to prepare us her best meal."

"Hear! Hear!" said the rest.

"Anyone for a game of Pick-Up Sticks?" said Winslow.

The dinner was planned for six o'clock the following evening. That morning the little room bounced from floor to floor as the Wilsons slipped invitations under the doors of the dinner guests. After ordering the dinner menu in the hotel kitchen, they returned to Otis to prepare the room.

"Well, we don't need to buy any flowers," said Walter.

"But the room can use a good cleaning," said Winona.

By now the Wilsons had made friends with the maids on the sixth, eleventh, and twenty-eighth floors. For an hour these kind women scurried around the little room, vacuuming the rug, dusting the furniture, bringing in extra chairs, polishing the button panel, and wiping fingerprints from the full-length mirror.

At five-thirty, a blond man with one gold earring entered the little room. He was pushing a large cart.

"My name is Sydney, and I will be your waiter this evening," he said with an Italian accent.

Sydney spread a linen tablecloth on the table. He laid out fine china, sterling silverware, a candle in a silver holder, and cloth napkins rolled into silver napkin rings. Finally, with a click of his heels, he stood in a corner with a towel over his arm.

"Excellent job, young man," said Walter.

Sydney nodded crisply. "During the day I'm really an actor," he said, this time with a German accent. "In the evening I practice how to act like a waiter."

At a quarter to six, Walter began pushing buttons. Otis moved from floor to floor collecting the guests.

Mr. Brown stepped in on the twenty-fourth floor. He handed the twins two baseball caps. Each had a visor on the back as well as the front. "Here's a fad I tried selling last week," Mr. Brown said. "Some kids wear caps with visors in front, some with visors pointing backward. So I figured caps with visors going both ways would please everyone. But I still have suitcases full of them. No kidding. The fad isn't catching on too well."

On the top floor Mrs. Goldengate entered. Oui-Oui yapped in her arms. "My, my, I'm grateful for this invitation," she said. "How refreshing it is not having to rush to dinner. Tonight my dining place came right to me."

Next the little room dropped to the lobby. Cathy stepped out of her flower stall to join the group. She wore a short black dress and black tights. Her hair was piled high on her head. "How wonderful," she said. "I haven't been out to dinner in months."

Gavin arrived soon afterward. The teenager looked different dressed in a corduroy jacket and chino pants. His hair was slicked back and his brown loafers wore a shine.

The doors slid shut and Otis rose.

"Splendid. Everyone has arrived," said Walter. "Please have a seat."

The diners squeezed in around the table. Walter lifted a bottle of champagne from an ice bucket. "Only the best," he said, twisting off the cork.

Pop!

The cork shot to the ceiling. Walter poured

a glass for each guest. The twins had apple juice.

Ping! Ping! Ping! went Walter's fork against his glass.

"I propose a toast," he said. "Here's to a fine evening with our friends."

The group clinked glasses together. "Hear! Hear!" they chanted.

Gavin and Cathy sat side by side on a trunk. Gavin looked at Cathy and blushed. Cathy looked at Gavin and smiled. Gavin stared down at his fingernails, wishing they were cleaner.

A Top 10 tune floated down from the overhead speaker.

"Great music," said Whitney.

"Fantabulous," said Winslow.

"Something tells me you chose the music for tonight, Gavin," said Winona.

"Well, sure," said the teenager. "I wanted something special."

Cathy looked around the room. "So, Gavin, this is where you've been taking all the flowers you bought from me. I thought . . . I thought . . ."

Winona quickly interrupted. "I bet you thought Gavin was buying the flowers for some girl. But every day he brought them to us to make our home brighter."

Sydney snapped into action. "Tonight Chef Michelle has prepared an exquisite meal, especially for this unique compact dining room," he said with a French accent. "We begin with a shrimp salad made with little leaves of lettuce, tiny tomatoes, mini-mushrooms, and shrimpy shrimp."

Walter patted his stomach. "Double portions for me," he said. "Let us eat."

Sydney served the salads. As he circled the table, turning a three-foot-long pepper grinder over each one, Otis suddenly jerked to a stop. The lights went out and the speakers went silent. Low rumbling filled the room. The walls began to rattle.

Oui-Oui yapped in Mrs. Goldengate's arms. "My, my," the woman said. "I do believe we're having an earthquake."

The group sat in the dark without saying a word. The little room continued to shake. Wires sang overhead. Creaks and grinding noises came from under the floor. After a final jolt, everything became perfectly still.

Walter struck a match and lit the candle on the table. The light bathed the entire room in a soft golden glow.

"Splendid," he said. "The shaker appears to be over."

"No one is hurt," said Winona. "Not a thing was damaged."

Whitney pressed the *L* button on the wall. Nothing happened. She pressed the rest of the buttons and the room remained motionless.

"Otis must be stuck between floors," said Gavin. "That happened the last time we lost power in the hotel."

Winslow picked up the white telephone. "The phone is dead as well," he announced.

"No matter. We're all in good company," said Walter. "Sydney, pour us some more champagne."

By candlelight, the Wilsons and their guests finished their meal of *petit* pork chops, baby peas, and slivers of apple pie à la mode. Afterward they played Pick-Up Sticks.

During the game, Walter told a story about his family's vacation the previous summer. "It was getting late, you see, and we were looking for a place to spend the night. Just as the sun went down, we spotted twenty or so small wooden cabins scattered about a field. Each cabin was about the size of this room, ideal for our family.

"Winona and I entered one of the cabins while the twins went to find the owner. I was just about to light a match to see what was inside when Winslow came running in. He was screaming like a playground whistle. Remember that, son?"

Winslow, who was about to pinch a yellow Pick-Up Stick, nodded. "I sure do," he said. "I had just read a sign that said 'No Trespassing: Property of Hudson Fireworks Company.'"

"Those little cabins were where they made

fireworks," said Whitney. "That vacation almost turned into a real blast."

The company exchanged glances and laughed nervously.

Meanwhile, Winona noticed that Gavin and Cathy still weren't talking. "So, Gavin," she said. "You mentioned that you were working at this hotel to save money for college."

Gavin blushed. "Sure, Mrs. Wilson," he said.

"Well, young man, a college education is a fine thing," said Walter. "What do you plan to study?"

"Education. I want to be a teacher," the teenager answered. "I want to teach young children."

"Excellent profession, son," said Mr. Brown. "No kidding. Just think of the long summer vacations you can spend with your family."

"And what could be more valuable in our cities than a good teacher?" asked Mrs. Goldengate.

Cathy looked at Gavin and smiled.

There followed a lively conversation about colleges and teachers. The group was chattering away when a knock came from overhead. Oui-Oui yapped.

Walter held up his hands to silence his guests.

The knock came again. Everyone looked up toward the trapdoor in the ceiling.

"Are you down there?" said a voice. "Mr. Wilson? Mrs. Wilson? Are you okay?"

"It's Joe, the night watchman," said Winona. "Joe's up there."

"Joe, good fellow, come on down," said Walter. "We're in the middle of an excellent party. Only the best. There's room for another guest."

"The entire city has lost power, Mr.

Wilson," the night watchman called down. "I've come to take you out."

"That's very kind of you, Joe," Winona said to the ceiling. "But there's no need to go through the trouble. All is well down here."

"No kidding. This beats being back in my lonely room," said Mr. Brown.

"No power? How delightful," said Mrs. Goldengate. "Now I couldn't rush out anywhere even if I had to."

"This sure beats waiting on ornery customers in the restaurant," said Sydney with a Scottish accent.

Cathy and Gavin exchanged glances and smiled.

"Suit yourselves, folks," said Joe. "But the power won't be on for at least two hours."

Walter grabbed a fistful of Pick-Up Sticks and dropped them on the table. "Splendid," he said. "That gives us time for many more rounds. Care to join us, Joe?"

"No, thanks, Mr. Wilson. I need to find people who want to be rescued. So long, folks. Drop down to the basement for a visit soon."

The next morning Walter awoke with a chocolate mint stuck to his right cheek. Soon after the lights had gone back on the night before, the guests had left. Sydney had cleared the dishes, and the eleventh-floor maid had put fresh linen on the trunk-beds. She had left a chocolate mint on each pillow, as was the hotel's custom. Finally she had ridden the little room from the top floor to the lobby. Outside Otis's doors on each floor, she'd hung a Do Not Disturb sign, so that the family could sleep late.

Now Walter sat at the breakfast table, wiping the brown glob off with a napkin. "I never saw the little treat on my pillow before I unscrewed the lightbulb," he said.

After breakfast Winona picked up her sketchbook and the twins their paperbacks.

Walter opened his newspaper. "Since this is our final full day in Otis, I say we spend it quietly sitting right here," he suggested.

As he spoke, two men entered the little room. One had a thin goatee. The other had large ears with hair sprouting from them. They both wore dark sunglasses and shiny black suits. Between them they carried a large trunk.

Walter laid down the paper. "Top of the morning, gentlemen," he said. "Guests are always welcome in our home."

"Right, Pops," said the bearded man.

"Jeez!" muttered the big-eared man. "This city is filled with weirdos."

The doors opened on the sixteenth floor. The men, lugging their trunk, stepped out.

"Two men and only one trunk," Winslow noted.

"Very mysterious," said Whitney.

Walter snapped the newspaper in his hands. "Mysterious indeed," he said. "Look at the morning headlines."

Winona, Winslow, and Whitney looked up to read the large print:

GIRL MISSING
TODAY SAN FRANCISCO POLICE REPORTED THE DISAPPEARANCE OF LIZZY CHRONICLE, 10-YEAR-OLD DAUGHTER OF BILLIONAIRE FRANK CHRONICLE, PUBLISHER OF THIS NEWSPAPER.

Ten minutes later the doors of the little room opened in the lobby. Gavin entered, wearing a grin and a crooked bow tie. He pulled in the room service cart, then pressed the button for the sixteenth floor.

"You look chipper this morning, young man," said Walter.

"And you haven't brought us any flowers today," said Winona.

"I feel on top of the world, Mr. Wilson, Mrs. Wilson," said the bellhop. "I feel lighter than air."

"I feel that way when Otis goes downward," said Winslow.

Walter studied the food cart. "Another meal for us already, young man?"

"No, sir," said Gavin. "This is room service for two new arrivals on the sixteenth floor."

"But there are three plates on the cart," said Winona.

"The two men ordered two plates of scrambled eggs and a hamburger," said Gavin. "So that's what I'm bringing them."

"Very mysterious," said Whitney.

That afternoon, as the little room sat in the lobby, Cathy stepped out from her flower stall.

"Guess what?" she said to the Wilsons. "Gavin stopped by my counter. And guess what? Instead of buying flowers, he talked to me. And guess what? He asked me out to a movie on Friday."

"Splendid," said Walter. "By the way, young lady, did you notice Gavin delivering any food to the sixteenth floor around noon?"

"That's where he was headed when he stopped by," the girl answered. "He had two BLTs and a hamburger."

Winslow looked over his paperback. "Another odd hamburger," he said.

"Things are even more mysterious," said Whitney.

The Wilsons chose to dine in again that

evening. Mr. Brown brought the evening newspaper and some Chinese food in small white boxes.

"Dinner is on me tonight," he said. "No kidding. It's great having a friendly family to share a meal with."

As the group ate, the salesman heard about the hamburger mystery.

"First the two men arrive with one trunk," said Walter, fumbling with his chopsticks.

"And they were very rude," said Winona.

Winslow slurped some noodles. "And we can't figure out what the men are doing with the extra food," he said.

"It's all very mysterious," said Whitney.

"No kidding. Sounds like they have a third person in the room," said Mr. Brown. "Did you see the evening headlines?"

He held up the newspaper. The headlines were even more alarming than the previous ones:

LIZZY CHRONICLE
REPORTED KIDNAPPED
$10 MILLION RANSOM
DEMANDED

Everyone read their fortune cookies in silence. Mr. Brown got off on the twenty-fourth floor, and immediately the little room started downward. In the lobby Gavin entered, humming to himself. Again he pushed in the room service cart. He looked into the full-length mirror and began combing his hair.

"Is there a hamburger on one of those plates, young man?" Walter asked.

"Sure," Gavin said. "Two steaks and a hamburger."

"And is that food for the men on the sixteenth floor?" said Winslow.

The teenager nodded.

"And I'll bet anything that extra hamburger is for Lizzy Chronicle," said Whitney.

Gavin lowered his comb. "Lizzy

Chronicle? You mean the girl who was kidnapped?"

"We believe she's here in this hotel," said Winona. "Poor thing."

Walter pulled out his suspenders with his thumbs. "It all adds up," he said. "The men on the sixteenth floor must be the kidnappers who kidnapped that kid. Young man, would you mind stalling that room service delivery a minute? I have a plan to find out if our suspicions are correct."

12

Walter snapped his suspenders and raised a finger. Winona, Winslow, Whitney, and Gavin leaned forward to hear his plan.

"First, we compose a note," he said. He raised another finger. "Second, we place the note under the hamburger." A third finger went up. "Next, Lizzy reads the note that tells her to give us a signal that she's there."

He raised a fourth finger. "Finally, we receive her signal and call the police on our white phone."

"But what if Lizzy isn't in the room and the men read the note?" asked Gavin. "Won't you be in a tight spot?"

"Young man, we are the Wilsons, and we've been in many tight spots," said Walter.

The little room started going upward.

"And we rise to the occasion," said Winslow.

Winona tore a piece of paper out of her sketchbook and pulled a pencil from behind her ear. "I'll compose the note," she said. She wrote:

Lizzy,
   If you are in the room, turn this note over. Leave it under the plate. Help will come.
       From the Wilsons in the
       Otis Room

Each Wilson signed the note, and Gavin slipped it under the hamburger. When the doors opened on the sixteenth floor, he stepped out, shrugging.

"Good luck, young man," Walter called after him.

"You're our hero, dear," Winona said.

"Go for it, Gavin," said the twins.

The family leaned out of Otis. They watched the teenager push the trolley down the hall. He knocked on a door at the end. The door opened just wide enough for a hairy arm to reach out and pull the cart into the room.

"That's how it is every meal," Gavin said when he had returned to the little room. "No one says a word. And I never see a thing inside the room. The food cart is waiting in the hall a half hour later."

"Splendid," said Walter. "That gives me time to finish this crossword puzzle before the action begins."

The Wilsons took Gavin to the lobby. They waited there while thirty minutes clicked away on the clock behind the reception desk. When the bellhop returned, they escorted him back to the sixteenth floor.

In no time the cart, piled with dirty dishes, stood again in the little room.

Walter wiggled his fingers. "The moment of truth," he said. "Let's see what's under the hamburger plate. Since I'm the oldest, I'll do the honors."

"Ladies before gentlemen," said Winona. "I'll lift it."

"Children first," said the twins. And the four Wilsons lifted the plate together.

There sat the paper. A message written on it in sloppy handwriting read:

Yes, I am here. And I'm bored. I'm sick of eating hamburgers, and the TV gets only twenty-seven channels. Get me out of here!!!!
     Lizzy

Immediately Walter reached for the white phone. "Hello, Mrs. Quinn," he said. "Get me the police."

14

After Walter had called the police, he pushed the *L* button. By the time the doors opened in the lobby, a dozen hefty policemen were standing there.

"Come on in," Walter said. "Step to the rear. Going up."

On the way to the sixteenth floor, the Wilsons explained the note to the officers.

When the doors opened, the police rushed into the hall.

Ten minutes later they were back. They held the elbows of the two men, who were both in handcuffs.

"It's you again, Pops," the man with the goatee said to Walter.

"Weirdos," muttered the big-eared man.

Accompanying them was a pouting, freckle-faced girl. She held a hamburger. "What took everyone so long?" she said. "I thought I'd never get rescued. That was so booooooring. Nothing to do. No games to play. No videos to watch." She took a big bite out of her burger.

When they reached the lobby, a swarm of reporters was waiting. Cameras clicked and whirred. Flashes went off. As the police led the two kidnappers into a waiting squad car, the reporters surged into Otis. They thrust microphones toward the Wilsons, shouting questions.

Walter ran a hand over his thinning hair. "You are all welcome!" he shouted. "There is always room in our home for more visitors."

The hotel manager, who showed up shortly, was delighted with all the free publicity the Wilsons' rescue had brought the hotel.

"In appreciation for what you've done," he told the family, "I would like to offer you the use of our Presidential Suite for the remainder of your stay."

"Thank you very much," said Walter. "But we prefer to stay in Otis our last night."

"We'd be lost in a large suite," said Winona.

"And it doesn't even move," said Winslow.

"How would we meet people stuck on one floor?" asked Whitney.

The Wilsons rose extra early the next morning. They began packing their trunks. They returned the table and chairs to their proper floors. Winona removed her sketches from the walls, and Walter took down the Home Sweat Home sampler.

At seven o'clock Gavin arrived with the morning newspaper and breakfast. He held up the front page. A picture of the Wilsons filled the top half.

"Now, that's what I call one great-looking family," said Walter.

"But your shirttail is hanging out, Walter," said Winona.

"And Winslow is giving me bunny ears," said Whitney.

After breakfast Mr. Brown paid a visit. A dab of shaving cream jiggled beneath one sideburn.

"I just read about you people in the newspaper," he announced. "Your picture gave me an idea. Why couldn't this family become the latest fad? We'll call you the Elevator Family. We can sell Elevator Family dolls and Elevator Family books. There will be Elevator Family lunch boxes, Elevator Family sweatshirts, and coming soon—*The Elevator Family Movie*. This could be the idea I've been waiting for. If this fad catches on, I won't need to leave home anymore."

At that moment Mrs. Goldengate entered the little room. She wore a heavy coat. Oui-Oui, dressed in a red sweater, yapped in her arms.

"I'm rushing off," Mrs. Goldengate said.

"To brunch?" asked Winslow.

"To a meeting?" asked Whitney.

"My, my, no," said the woman. "I'm going to visit my children in Montana. Being with this family has reminded me of the good times I've had with my own. I hope to stay there and not rush anywhere for a long while."

At last the trunks were packed. For the final time, Walter pressed the *L* button. When the doors opened in the lobby, Gavin was leaning against the flower stall, chatting with Cathy. Walter cleared his throat loudly until the bellhop rushed over to help with the trunks.

"I sure never knew flowers could be so interesting," the teenager explained.

The Wilsons marched out of Otis in single file. Gavin followed with the luggage on a cart. Cathy called out a farewell. Mrs. Quinn, behind the reception desk, squinted and shook her head.

Roland opened the door. "Come again soon," he said.

Outside, Gavin stood the trunks on end. "Well, so long, Mr. Wilson, Mrs. Wilson, Whitney, and Winslow," he said. "Sure was great having you here. Where are you going next?"

"We never seem to know where we're going until we get there," said Walter.

"Maybe we can stay in one of those fantabulous little cabins I saw at the end of the Golden Gate Bridge," said Winslow. "People drive by and hand money to the people living inside."

At that moment a small yellow taxi drove up to the hotel entrance. After piling the luggage in the taxi's trunk, the four Wilsons squeezed into the backseat.

Walter rolled down the window. "But wherever we end up next, young man," he called to Gavin, "you know it will be the best. Because nothing less than the best will do."

Then, waving good-bye, the Elevator Family, packed in the back of the compact taxi, drove off.